WHITCHURCH-STOUFFVILLE PUBLIC LIBRARY
WITHDRAWN WS567700

SUPERHERO NINJA WRESTLING STAR

D1220780

LORNA SCHULTZ NICHOLSON

**James Lorimer & Company Ltd., Publishers
Toronto**

WHITCHURCH-STOUFFVILLE PUBLIC LIBRARY   JUN 2 0 2017

Copyright © 2017 by Lorna Schultz Nicholson
Published in Canada in 2017.

All rights reserved. No part of this book may be reproduced or transmitted in any form or by any means, electronic or mechanical, including photocopying, or by any information storage or retrieval system, without permission in writing from the publisher.

James Lorimer & Company Ltd., Publishers acknowledges the support of the Ontario Arts Council (OAC), an agency of the Government of Ontario, which in 2015-16 funded 1,676 individual artists and 1,125 organizations in 209 communities across Ontario for a total of $50.5 million. We acknowledge the support of the Canada Council for the Arts, which last year invested $153 million to bring the arts to Canadians throughout the country. This project has been made possible in part by the Government of Canada and with the support of the Ontario Media Development Corporation.

Cover design: Tyler Cleroux
Cover and interior images: Shutterstock, iStock

Library and Archives Canada Cataloguing in Publication

Schultz Nicholson, Lorna, author
    Superhero ninja wrestling star / Lorna Schultz Nicholson.

Issued in print and electronic formats.
ISBN 978-1-4594-1196-8 (paperback).--ISBN 978-1-4594-1198-2 (epub)

    I. Title.

PS8637.C58S96 2017   jC813'.6   C2016-906032-2
                                                C2016-906033-0

Published by: Distributed by:
James Lorimer & Company Ltd.,   Formac Lorimer Books
Publishers   5502 Atlantic Street
117 Peter Street, Suite 304   Halifax, NS, Canada
Toronto, ON, Canada   B3H 1G4
M5V 0M3
www.lorimer.ca

Printed and bound in Canada.
Manufactured by Friesens Corporation in Altona, Manitoba, Canada in January 2017.
Job #229625

To all boys in grade six. You're special.

CHAPTER ONE

BIG CHANGES!!

With my new black backpack on my shoulder, I walked out my front door. And I almost choked. I'm not kidding. For a second, I couldn't breathe.

No way. There was just no way.

My best friend Shamini had turned into a giant!

I hadn't seen her all summer, even though Shamini lived next door to me. I'd been sent to stay with my grandparents on a farm in the middle of nowhere. They had no Wi-Fi. I spent two months in the one spot in the world that doesn't get a Wi-Fi signal. My mother and father had to work, and they made a big deal about me not being old enough to babysit my younger brother, Marvin. I could have taken care of Marvin. Really, I could have. Even though he's taller than me.

Everyone is taller than me.

Especially Shamini. How could one person have grown that much in just two months?

When I was at my grandparents', I went to the library to use the Wi-Fi and stay connected with my friends. Lucky Shamini had spent a month in Europe. She sent me selfies of her standing in front of a lot of old churches. But this new height thing wasn't something I'd noticed. Maybe because the churches were so huge? How could one person, a single person, grow *that much* in one summer? It looked like she grew another foot.

I was pretty much the same height as when I left for my grandparents'.

"Hey, Archie!" Shamini called out to me. She ran across the yard, waving her arms and laughing. At least she was happy to see me!

I waved back. But I couldn't stop staring at her. She wore a pink dress and a jean jacket. Her black hair looked longer and shinier or . . . I don't know. Something was different. Whatever had happened to Shamini over the summer made her look really good though. But why was she wearing a jean jacket? It was boiling out. The sun was a big yellow ball, still pumping out summer heat.

"Hey, Shamini," I croaked. Yesterday, I *had* been excited for school. But now I sort of wished we had two more months of summer before grade six. I needed time to catch up or something.

Then she was standing right in front of me. Our difference in height became reality. She threw her arms around me and the top of my head was level with her shoulder. "I've missed you," she said.

"I missed you too." I pulled away and looked down at my shoes. They were the same ones I had at the end of grade five. Dad said that it was a waste of money to buy me new ones if the old ones still fit. Same went for the rest of my clothes. But when did I care what Shamini thought of my clothes? She's been one of my best friends since we were little.

"How was your *summer?*" She asked.

I kicked the ground. "Boring."

"Did you seriously have no Wi-Fi?"

I looked up and rolled my eyes. "So lame." I didn't want to tell her that my grandparents also had the smallest and oldest TV on the face of the planet. It weighed a ton, but had this little, squarish screen. Playing video games on it sucked big time. "I read a lot of comic books," I said, trying to sound cool. I had to change the subject. "Your summer looked amazing."

"It was," Shamini said. She put her hands to her face and closed her eyes. She kind of looked like the girls on TV when they thought a boy was cute. Why was she acting like a girl? It was one thing that she really *looked* like a girl now, but she was also *acting* like one.

But then she opened her eyes and put her fist up. I sighed in relief. I bumped it with mine, then we did our little hip hop groove move. That was our real thing. It made me feel like we hadn't changed. She hadn't changed.

"What was your favourite city?" I asked.

"Paris!!!!" She threw her arms in the air.

"Did you eat those long bread things?"

"Baguettes," she said. "I ate so many I thought I'd turn into one."

She almost has, I thought, looking at how long her legs were.

"I loved them, and the gelato in Italy," she went on.

I'd never had gelato. Ice cream, sherbet, but not gelato. It sounded foreign and expensive. We didn't do expensive in our house. We did Chinese noodles. And ice cream from a plastic pail. In case I forgot to mention, my name is Archie Zheng. The Zheng part is because my great-grandparents came from China. Thus the height thing, and the Chinese noodles. Shamini's mom was South Asian and her father was this super tall blondish man. My mom loved to say that Shamini got the best of both. Me, I got the worst of both — my dad's skinny build and my grandmother's height. She wasn't even five feet tall.

A squeaking sound made me turn around. My other best friend Alfie screeched to a stop on his clunky old bike. "Hel-lo, grade six! Hey, Archie, Shamini. What are you guys talking about?"

Alfie, Shamini and I had hung around together since kindergarten. I looked at Alfie — *up* at Alfie. He'd grown too. Up and *out*. Alfie didn't need to grow out as much as up. His face looked like a big round basketball spotted with a gazillion freckles. His brown, curly hair sat like a mushroom on top of his head. Standing beside him, I felt small. Like really small. Like really, really small. What was happening?

Grade six was happening.

"We were talking about Paris." Shamini waved her arms around and her dark brown eyes were sparkling or something. "And the baguettes."

"Doesn't look like Archie ate a bag of anything." Alfie rocked his rickety bike back and forth and it made squealing noises. The ripped seat, rusty chain and ratty streamers (yes, streamers) made the bike a wreck.

"Not him," said Shamini. "Me. I ate baguettes. In Paris."

"Your chain needs oiling," I said. Enough of this baguette talk. They were skinny bread things. I didn't need to be reminded about skinny.

Shamini checked her phone. "Hey, we'd better get going. Don't want to be late!"

Between my two friends, I wondered if I looked like the shrimp in the middle. What if everyone in my grade six class had grown over the summer? My stomach felt queasy and

I wanted to puke up the two eggs my mother made me eat. She said they were good for me, good protein for growth. I don't think eating the whole dozen would have made much difference this morning.

CHAPTER TWO
GIRL CHANGES

On the way to school, things sort of got back to the way they used to be. We talked about the summer, Shamini's trip and incredible soccer camp. Alfie's gazillion science, superhero and comic book camps. My boredom.

Shamini said, "I hope our new teacher is nice." She started taking off her jean jacket. "It's so hot out," she exclaimed as she tied it around her waist.

I wished Shamini had left her coat on. Because when she took it off, I stared. Then I saw Alfie staring, bug-eyed. Was I looking that creepy too?

I felt him nudge me. "Wow!" He mouthed.

I frowned at him. Then I made a slashing motion across my throat.

Shamini had not just grown in height. She'd grown somewhere else. The place where girls grow. You know, around the chest. And she looked good. Too good. Suddenly, to me anyway, she looked like one of the girls on the Bollywood shows that Shamini's mom was always watching. All I'd watched all summer was WWE wrestling because of my grandfather. When the girl wrestlers came on, my grandmother told my grandfather to turn the television off. They didn't wear a lot of clothes.

"I think I'm going to go out for the soccer team," said Shamini, tossing back her hair. With her jacket off, I could see how long her hair had grown. Like all the way down her back. It glowed. And her skin glowed or something too. I kind of didn't like that she looked different. What was happening here?

"Um, what soccer team?" I asked, trying to get the normal back.

"The school team for grade sevens and eights. My soccer coach at camp said I should try out for something that would challenge me. Sometimes they take a few grade sixes."

"Cool," said Alfie.

"You guys going out for any teams?" she asked.

"Us!" Alfie laughed almost spitting at the same time. "Not a chance. We're like the worst athletes ever."

"I haven't played any sport since T-ball," I laughed. But no one else did, so I guess it wasn't funny.

"You used to be able to run fast," Shamini said to me. "Join cross-country. It's always the skinny guys who can run fast."

Ouch. *Skinny*. That hurt.

"How about we join a gaming team," said

NINJA!

Alfie. "We're fantastic at moving our thumbs."

"Pleeeeeease don't tell me you played video games all summer," said Shamini.

"Nope. I didn't," I said. "I got to watch wrestling with my grandfather. How lame is that? When I got sick of that, Marvin and I played ninjas or spies or superheroes outside."

"Ninjas and superheroes?" She frowned at me.

I shrugged. "Nothing else to do."

Suddenly her face broke out into a huge grin. "But spies are definitely okay. Did you guys see *Jimmy Bond?* He is *soooo cute*, and has the coolest gadgets."

"I saw it," said Alfie. "It was cool. I liked his laser-beam sunglasses. They burn through metal!"

Stuck at my grandparents', I didn't get to see the *Jimmy Bond* movie that had hit the theatres in July. Jimmy Bond was a teen billionaire and he had the best cars, clothes and hi-tech gadgets. "There's no movie theatre where my grandparents live," I said.

"That sucks," said Shamini.

When did my whole life start sucking? Thankfully, we were almost at the school. I had to get the morning going in a better direction.

Kids were still hanging around outside, so we weren't late. Little kids played on the playground, and the big kids just looked cool. Our school went up to grade eight, so we were past the middle, but not yet the big kids. And I mean big. By the way, the grade sevens and eights were looking *huge*. Shamini picked up her pace and it was hard to keep up to her long strides.

"There's Dylan and Sam," she said. She was almost running now.

"Who cares?" Alfie whispered to me.

Obviously, Shamini did. Dylan and Sam were in our grade. They played hockey and wore cool hockey jackets in the winter. Today they just had t-shirts on. Team sort of t-shirts. I think they lived in nice houses, but I wasn't 100 per cent sure, because I'd never been invited over. As Shamini ran toward them, she unwrapped her coat and put it on. Even though the temperature was rising, not falling, she buttoned it up. That made me happy for some reason. Her hair flew behind her, and the sun shining on it made it sparkle. That made me sad for some reason.

Alfie nudged me. "She's wearing a bra! She's sure changed."

"Nah," I said. "She's still Shamini."

I hoped that was true. What if more than Shamini's size and shape had changed? What if she had changed her mind about friends? About me? When we were little we'd promised each other we would go to our first dance together. And grade six was the year for that first dance.

CHAPTER THREE

NOTHING TO DO

The bell rang. Alfie and I made our way into the class hoping to get a seat at the back. No go. Our new teacher said her name was Mrs. Golden. She didn't look golden at all, more like grey. She told us she had made a seat plan. What? Really?

I was glad to see I ended up sitting across from Shamini. Dylan was ahead of Shamini and Sam was on the other side of the room. Poor Alfie was in the front row. I think Alfie must have been discussed in the staff room before Mrs. Golden took over for Mrs. Caldwell, who had a baby. Alfie talked a lot and disrupted the class a lot. Oh, and bugged the teacher a lot. It would take him about a half a day to drive Mrs. Golden crazy if she kept him at the front.

Mrs. Golden told us all to quiet down. Nobody really listened.

Then she asked in a sort of loud voice, "How many of you like wrestling?"

It was such a weird thing for a new teacher to ask on the first day of school. Everyone stopped talking. We just stared at her.

"Thank you for your attention," she said, smiling. "Now, about my wrestling comment. I'm going to be starting a wrestling club at this school. My husband was a college wrestler and is going to help me coach."

Wrestling? After the summer with my grandfather, I knew wrestling. But Mrs. Golden? I couldn't put together the old lady standing in front of me with the hugely muscled guys in wild costumes.

"I'm hoping some of you will join," she said. "Now, I'd like to talk about my class rules."

She talked about washroom breaks and eating

and chewing gum. She talked about no phones, no phones, no phones and more no phones. I zoned out. I didn't have a phone. I wanted one though, for my birthday on September 26. Not everyone had one, I got that. But both Shamini and Alfie had one because their parents liked to text them. The plans cost too much, according to my mother. But maybe a phone might make me look older and cooler? I would have to beg.

I stared at my classmates. The only other kid who hadn't grown was Susie Wong. But she had an excuse. She'd skipped a grade and had a December birthday and was still smarter than all of us. And I had maybe a centimetre on Susie. And it wasn't like *I* had a December birthday like Alfie. Shamini had hers way last January, so she was way ahead of everyone.

Mrs. Golden had a lot of rules. I was able to think about my birthday on and off until recess. Every year I had a birth-day party at my house, "to keep the costs down." Last year I'd begged my mother for a laser tag party or paint ball, or even going to a movie. If I had a cool party everyone would come. She said no. I had to have it at the house. And since it was at the house, only half of the kids showed up. Then after my party, all the guys who had come talked about how lame it was. This year couldn't be a repeat of that.

When the recess bell went, Alfie and I walked outside together. Shamini sort of waited for us. But then Dylan showed up and she went off with him. He was one of the kids who didn't come to my party last year.

What was with Shamini? The three of us used to hang out at recess. When we were in like grade two and three we loved playing in the jungle gym area. Others had played with us too. Now, there seemed to be little groups all over the place. Alfie and me were like this group of two.

Alfie said, "Goldie-Oldie is going to kill us."

"That was pretty boring," I said.

"And what about her wrestling program." He rolled his eyes. "What would she know about WWE? No one's going to join. Parents will put up a big stink. The only good thing would be the girls wearing those outfits. And why am I at the front?"

"Front of what?" I said, totally distracted. Across the playground I could see Shamini had her jacket off and was talking to Naomi and Rachelle. I tried not to think about her front and the fact that she now wore a . . . a . . . bra. Even thinking the word was weird. We didn't talk about those kinds of things in my house. And weirder that the word was lumped together with Shamini. Alfie must have seen I wasn't paying attention, because he nudged me.

"Recess is boring," he said, looking around.

None of the grade sixes were playing on the playground equipment. The girls were all talking. Dylan and Sam were playing soccer with boys who were good at sports and bigger. Of course, everyone was bigger. Was that how it was going to be at recess from now on? Were we supposed to be grown up?

"What should we do?" Alfie asked, shoving his hands in his pockets.

"I dunno."

"I wanna play superheroes," he said. "Or ninjas or something fun."

"I don't think that's a good idea." I paused before I said, "Let's go talk to Shamini."

"She's with Naomi," said Alfie, moaning. "Naomi hates me."

"No, she doesn't. Not anymore. Or I don't think she does." I started walking toward Shamini.

Alfie huffed beside me. "I didn't mean for the gum to get stuck in her hair. And I told her it looked good short once it was cut out. I don't know why she still hates me. Hey, *Surge* is starting again this Friday. Wanna watch it together?"

Surge was a TV show about a guy who was the fastest runner in the galaxy. He used his speed to save the world, and the girls, of course. When he was a teenager he was trying to run away from some bad guys when he got zapped by a meteorite. It gave him superhuman speed.

He could run away from any bad guy, and win the battle, because he was fast. Alfie and I watched it every Friday night.

Friday seemed a long way away. We were only at morning recess on Tuesday. "Sure," I said about Friday night. So far I had nothing else to do. One day of grade six and already I was as bored as the whole summer made me.

We were walking toward Shamini when I felt a soccer ball hit me on the back. It almost knocked me over. "What the —" I yelled.

CHAPTER FOUR

COULD I BE FAST?

I turned to see Adam and Carey heading toward me. They were like the kings of grade seven. No one messed with them. They wore cool khaki shorts and baseball hats backwards. I picked up the ball and tried to throw it back to them. I watched it go sky-high in the wrong direction.

"You throw like a girl," said Adam, howling like a mean monkey. I noticed they were both taller, way taller even than Shamini.

"Uh oh," whispered Alfie.

Within seconds they were looming over me. Their shadows covered me.

"Don't ever touch my ball again," said Adam.

"I can't help it if it hit me," I said.

Adam gave me a little push with his finger. "I said . . . don't touch my ball again."

"Sorry," I said.

"Yeah, he's sorry," said Alfie.

"Shut up, dough-boy. Go eat another doughnut."

I saw Alfie's cheeks redden. Adam gave me one more little push before he turned and walked away. "Next time we won't be so nice," said Carey over his shoulder.

"I hate those guys," said Alfie when they were out of earshot. I could tell by his voice that he was trying not to cry. "Wouldn't it be awesome to be like Surge and be able to run away from them? Leave them in the dust wondering how we got away so fast. Then dart around them with their ball and have their heads spinning."

"Yeah," I said. "But we're not superhuman."

Fortunately, the bell rang. First time in my life I was glad recess was over. Alfie nattered on and on about being superhuman as we walked across the school yard. Then he asked, "You know what *you* need to do?"

"What?"

"Actually be someone like Surge. Okay, so you're puny. And not superhuman. But that doesn't mean you can't run fast like him."

"Why me? It's your idea."

"No, no. This is a much better thing for you to do. Skinny kids are always the best runners. Even Shamini said that." Alfie was talking fast, really fast. "If you were fast you could run away and they wouldn't catch you. This is something that is doable for you. I think we need to work on you, train you. I could be like your coach. This would be fun! If nothing else it will give us something to do!"

Walking back to class, I wondered if Alfie was right.

Mrs. Golden made us all sit down right away. Then she told us to take out our notebooks. We were going to do work on the first day of school? I opened my book and stared down at the white page. My vision blurred, like Surge did when he ran. I tuned out Mrs. Golden and started doodling. Surge was not real tall. Like me. And he was skinny. Like me. But he was fast. Could I be fast? I doodled and doodled until I felt a wave of warm air over me. I looked up and there was Mrs. Golden.

"What is your name?" she asked me.

"Archie."

"Well, Archie, in my class we save our art-work for art. Right now we are not doing art." She held up my paper. "This is pretty good. I don't think I've heard of . . . Surge."

The entire class burst out laughing.

"He's really fast," blurted out Alfie from the front of the room. "Like super fast. Like he zooms and is crazy fast. He runs away from the bad guys."

Now everyone was really laughing.

"Really," said Mrs. Golden. She held up her hand to get everyone to quiet down. "I guess I'm not quite up to *speed* on these characters."

Everyone laughed at her lame joke, except me. I slouched and slid down my desk, lowering my head so no one could see my red face. It was burning and so were the tips of my ears. Mrs. Golden put my notebook back on my desk. "This is well done, Archie. Just save it for later, okay."

I didn't answer. I couldn't. Mrs. Golden turned and started to walk up to the front. Dylan turned around and whispered, "Really mature, Archibald."

For no reason, except I was embarrassed, I blurted out, "Shut it." The words came out much louder than I wanted them to. I guess I was just so mad at being small, and now babyish too.

Mrs. Golden turned around. "Did you just tell me to *shut it*?"

I couldn't say that I was talking to Dylan because that would be like squealing, so I just lowered my head and stared at my desk. Plus, I had this lump in my throat and would probably squeak when I talked.

"Maybe you need a little cool down in the hall."

The hall? I'd never been sent to the hall before. Was I supposed to just go? Was she going to tell me to go? I slowly lifted my head. She pointed to the door. Okay, I got it. I slunk out. The hallway was super quiet and I tried to breathe. What was I supposed to do out here? A part of me wanted to cry. But that would make me look like a real *baby*. That would be the absolute worst. I leaned against the wall. Grade six was not starting out the way I'd planned. Even being at my grandparents' was better than this.

"Excuse me."

I looked up and saw a teacher. He wasn't a teacher I knew. "What are you doing in the hall?" he asked.

I couldn't answer.

He pointed to the door leading to the grade five classroom. "You should go back to class. Or maybe you're in grade four." Now he pointed down the hall to the grade FOUR classroom.

I shook my head. "Um, I'm in grade six. I'm, um, doing something, um, for my teacher."

"Really? Okay." He walked away from me, his sneakers squeaking on the freshly waxed floor. I slid down the wall until my butt was on the ground. Grade five?! Are you kidding me? He thought I was in grade five?! Or even grade four. Was he joking? Something inside of me shrunk, like a balloon deflating, in one huge hiss. I had to do something about my size.

CHAPTER FIVE
GETTING WORSE, FAST

"Surge is the only way to go," said Alfie.

It was Friday and we were watching an old *Surge* episode in my living room. Our house only had a living room. Shamini's mom redid their house and now they had both a living room AND a family room.

The week had finally ended, and I felt this huge relief. So far I hated grade six. After being sent out to the hall on the first day, I'd made myself quiet in class. But that also made me like a geek. And a dweeb. And small. And a nothing. And small. And smaller. And smallest. But I didn't want to be embarrassed in front of the whole class again.

"You can't just mope around all year," Alfie said.

"Why not? Until I grow it would be the best thing."

"Well, for starters, it's no fun. And you'll miss the grade six dance. I've been practising my moves."

"So. Who cares about a stupid dance?" Shamini and I hadn't talked about the dance after Mrs. Golden mentioned it on Thursday. Dylan and Sam were taking up a lot of Shamini's time. What if she went with one of them? I wouldn't be surprised if she forgot about a promise she made when we were little. When we were *both* little.

"Come on," said Alfie. "At least making you like Surge will give us a mission. Surge is cool. He's like the best superhero ever. Treat it as a makeover."

"A what?"

"You know, one of those makeover things that my mother does when she goes to the hairdresser." He pointed to the TV screen. "What season should we start with?"

"One," I replied. If we started at the beginning it might give us enough time for Alfie to forget about his crazy idea.

I spread out on the sofa. Alfie sat up with a notebook in his hand.

"What are you doing?" I asked.

"Taking notes. If I'm gonna be your coach I need to set up a training plan."

Since we had nothing to do all weekend, I let Alfie go on about Surge. Most kids in our class were trying out for different things. Shamini was busy with the soccer thing. Her parents liked her in things. My parents thought homework was all I needed. Alfie's parents wanted him in things, but he refused.

"I'm going to ride my bike, Archie. I mean Surge," said Alfie. "And you'll run beside me."

It was kind of hard to run in high-top runners and jeans. But I did what he said. I made it to the first telephone pole before I stopped.

"This is tough," I said, panting.

"You need to work harder."

"I'd like to see you try it."

"I'm the coach. I don't have to. Anyway, I'd suck. You're skinny."

"Oh, that's helping me a lot, coach," I said, shaking my head. "Did you like look up TED talks on motivation?"

Alfie looked at his watch. "Five seconds and we go again."

Alfie told me to meet him after school on Monday outside by the track with my gym stuff on. No more street clothes, he said. I had done okay with the running on the weekend, so I agreed. Maybe I could be good? Just like Shamini said.

He shook his head when he saw me. "Surge wears aerodynamic clothing. That's your gym stuff from last year.

"So."

"Maybe I could steal some of Adriana's dance stuff for you. Or maybe not. It kind of has a lot of sparkly stuff on it."

Alfie had an older sister named Adriana and she would beat him over the head if he took her stuff. "I'm not wearing Adriana's clothes. I'm wearing my own. Should we get started?"

I had gone from running just one block to running five blocks. And it hadn't been all that bad. If I could do okay, maybe I could try out for the track team and then I could be somebody. Not just the skinniest kid in grade six.

We made our way over to the empty track. Clouds hid the sun and I liked that it was not sunny and bright.

"Once around for warm-up," said Alfie. "Then it will be time for you to run sprints. I did research and the best training is for you to run dashes."

"Let's just start with one lap," I said.

I got to the track and started running. At first it was easy. I felt good. I liked it. Maybe I could run cross-country. After my first lap, Alfie tried to call me over. But I didn't want to stop.

"I'm gonna run one more lap," I yelled to him.

I had just started the lap when I saw a big crowd of girls coming to the track. They were grade seven and eights except . . . Shamini. Oh no.

The girls started jogging around, and I picked up my pace. They had heard me say I was going to do a whole lap. If I bailed, they would wonder why. I had to finish the lap. Then I would leave. Run away.

I heard the footsteps behind me, getting closer and closer and closer. I picked up my pace. But that made my breath get heavier. I had to keep going. I tried to move my legs. Suddenly, there were feet beside me, surrounding me.

"What are you doing?" Shamini whispered.

"Training for cross-country." It was a lie. Why I lied, I don't know. But I did.

"You're going to try out?" She sounded excited. "That's awesome."

"Yeah." I tried to keep up with her. I heard more feet behind me. I tried to glance around, but it was like I was in the middle of a pack of race horses.

The girl up front turned around and ran backwards. "Okay, girls, let's pick it up!" She faced forward again and took off.

All the girls started running fast. Since I was in the middle of the pack, I picked up my speed too. My heart pounded through my t-shirt. Like crazy. The more I ran, the more I felt like my head was exploding. I saw stars. And meteorites. My heart felt like a bomb about to explode. I could hardly breathe or feel my body. Were my legs running on their own?

Up ahead I could see the finish line, or where the girls had started. My hope was that it was their finish line. One lap. I tried to glance at Shamini to see if she was breathing heavy like me, but she wasn't. She had a fierce look on her face. Okay, I could do fierce too.

We were almost there when the bossy girl said, "One more lap. We can do this!"

Another lap? I was dying. But Shamini was beside me. I had to prove myself. I kept running. And running. The stars got bigger and bigger.

I kept running. My heart beat faster and faster and faster.

And then I just couldn't breathe anymore. My chest was a ball of pain. My throat burned. My mouth was dry like someone had dumped sand in it. Stars now swam in front of me. And red circles. More red circles.

I had to stop. I just had to. So I did.

And a girl ran into me. "What'd you stop for?" she asked.

"I . . . I . . . can't breathe," I said. I bent over at the waist. My legs turned into gelatin and went totally wobbly. They buckled at the knees, and I fell to the ground.

CHAPTER SIX

HOPE FOR THE FUTURE

I heard a voice say, "I think he fainted."

"I didn't faint," I muttered.

"Can you hear me?" The girls' soccer coach stood over me. Her face looked weird and wobbly. I saw Shamini's face too. That made me close my eyes. Oh boy. This was embarrassing.

"Yes, I can hear you," I said. My face felt hot, really hot, like if I touched it my fingers would singe. It was probably really red too.

"That's good," said the coach. "Can you sit up?"

I put my hands on the dirt and pushed myself

up to a sitting position. I hung my head, not wanting to look at anyone, especially Shamini.

"I'm okay," I mumbled, staring at the ground, at the dirt and grass. There was no way I could look up. A bunch of girls were circling me.

"I think you should just sit for a few minutes." She handed me a water bottle and I took a drink. It tasted great.

"I think I'm just thirsty," I mumbled.

"You always need water to stay hydrated," she said.

I took another sip.

"Perhaps we should call your parents to pick you up."

"Ho-ly," said Alfie. Loudly too. Where had *he* come from? Why didn't he just stay back and let me handle this on my own.

"That was awesome," he said. "You were flying for a few seconds."

He turned to the coach and the girls. Oh no.

"Archie was training to be Surge," he said. "He was doing fantastic until he like passed out. There's hope for the future."

I groaned. Sometimes Alfie didn't know when to talk and when not to talk.

"Surge?" The coach shook her head.

"*Surge* is a stupid TV show for little kids," said one of the girls. It was the bossy one who had turned around and ruined everything. It was all her fault.

"It's not stupid," said Alfie. "Surge is like the coolest guy, because he is unbelievably fast."

I quickly glanced up and saw Shamini looking at me. Her eyebrows were almost touching because she was frowning *that much*. I forced myself to stand up. My legs almost buckled, but I managed to stay upright.

"The water helped," I muttered. "I can walk home. I live close." I didn't look at Shamini again.

"I'll take care of him," said Alfie. "I'm his coach."

44

"Okay," said the real coach. She handed me a water bottle. "Bring this back to school tomorrow."

I walked away, staring at the ground, ignoring the chatter going on behind me. My face was still burning. My legs felt like rubber instead of muscle. I was relieved to hear the coach tell the girls to listen up. I hoped they did too so they would stop staring at me.

"I can't believe you passed out like that," said Alfie. "But, man, you were a speedster!"

"Just keep walking," I mumbled.

All the way home, Alfie tried to talk about Surge. I let him babble on. By the time we hit my street, I had started to feel better, except for my face. It still burned.

We finally arrived at my house.

"Should we practise again tomorrow?" Alfie asked.

"No," I said.

"Okay. I'll think of something else then." He rode off on his squeaky bike.

What did he mean he'd think of *something else*?

We lived in a small three-bedroom house. Thankfully, I didn't have to share a room with Marvin. I managed to sneak past my mother, who was cooking dinner.

I slammed my door, flopped on my bed and stared at the ceiling. What a disaster. I never wanted to run ever again. I wanted to hide in my room for the rest of grade six and have my meals brought to me.

Of course, that didn't even last for ONE meal. Nope. My mom called to me from the kitchen to tell me dinner was ON THE TABLE.

I peeled myself off my bed. I hadn't moved in the half hour since I got home. I stood up and looked at myself in the mirror. I groaned. My arms were like strings. Skinny strings. My legs looked like twigs sticking out of my gym shorts.

I yanked on a pair of baggy sweats and the biggest sweat shirt I could find.

My dad was working late, so Marvin and I sat down at the kitchen table. Marvin rambled on and on about school. I kept my head down, shovelling food in my mouth. Was there any way I could make it go directly to my arms, my legs, my chest? Why couldn't the food make me grow right away?

"So, Archie," said my mother.

I looked up. "What?"

"About your birthday party. We should discuss it."

"I don't want a house party this year. Can we go to paint ball or laser tag?"

"It costs too much. I told you that last year."

I lowered my head. Just thinking about that party made me feel like a loser. Then it hit me. I had a great idea.

"How about," I said, "I just take a few friends to dinner? It could be pizza or something *cheap* like that?"

"How many is a few?"

"Shamini and Alfie?"

"And me," said Marvin.

"We could go to that *cheap* place called Bubba's," I said. I was on a roll. "All you can eat pizza and wings. It's super *cheap*. Last year you spent a fortune on food and got everyone a loot bag. This would be way less money." The loot bags had been the biggest joke of all. They had school supplies and dumb little games that were supposed to make you smarter.

"Are you sure that's what you want?" My mom kind of narrowed her eyes. "You had such fun last year."

Yeah right. "I was thinking," I said slowly,  "that if I had a *cheaper* party I could get a better gift." There, I'd said it.

"What kind of gift are you talking about?"

"A cell phone."

"Let me talk to your father."

My mother stood up and picked up her plate. "Let's get these dishes done, then homework."

She didn't say no.

CHAPTER SEVEN
THE RULE OF GRADE SIX

I was drying the dishes (because our dishwasher was broken) when the doorbell rang. Of course, Marvin ran to answer it to get out of helping me.

I heard Shamini's voice and felt my face heat up again. In fact, it felt like it was burning. I had to get to her before she started talking about what had happened at the track. My mother couldn't find out. I was moving toward the door when my mother said, "Archie, I'd like you to put the leftovers in this container."

"Sure," I said. "After I talk to Shamini."

She handed me the container anyway. "She'll come to the kitchen. She always does."

Shamini's hair was wet and she looked all shiny and clean. My skin was still crusted with sweaty salt. I hadn't showered. Instead, I'd stayed in my room, moping on my bed.

"Hello Shamini," said my mother. "It's so nice to see you."

"Hi, Mrs. Zheng," said Shamini. My mom and Shamini were pals. My mom had taught her to make chicken balls, a recipe she got off a TV cooking show. Shamini thought it was some ancient family recipe.

They chatted for a few seconds, while I tried to get Shamini's attention. When Shamini finally glanced my way, she said, "I came over to see if you were okay."

Too late! "I'm fine," I mumbled.

"Why would you ask if he is okay?" My mother was like a mosquito, buzzing around, looking for blood.

"Didn't he tell you?" I tried to get Shamini's attention again, but she was looking at my mom. If Shamini would glance my way, I would let her know to zip it. But that didn't happen. "He was practising for cross-country running today. But he ran too hard *and* didn't drink enough water. He kinda passed out."

"Cross-country?" I could feel my mother's eyes burning little holes in my skin. "You passed out? Why didn't you tell me?" She walked over to me and put her hand on my forehead. "You seem okay now."

I backed away from her. "I just didn't drink enough water," I said through a clenched jaw.

"We could train together," said Shamini. "It might help you make the team."

"Um, maybe," I said. *That* was a definite no.

Shamini glanced at her phone. "I guess I should get going," she said. "I still have home-work to do."

"It was nice to see you, Shamini," said my mother.

"See Mom," I said, pointing to Shamini's phone. "If I had a phone I'd know when to do homework."

"I said I would talk to your father."

Shamini's phone pinged. "It's my mom," she said. "She wants me to come home."

I walked Shamini to the door.

"You getting a phone for your birthday?" She nudged me with her shoulder.

I crossed my fingers and held them up. "Hope so. But then I might just have a small birthday party," I said. "Maybe a dinner at Bubba's. Um, would you come?"

"Of course. I love Bubba's. I heard that a guy just won a *hundred dollars* for eating one hundred chicken wings. Can you imagine? Eating that many chicken wings," she shook her head. "But getting a hundred dollars would be so cool."

"That's a lot of wings," I said.

"Hey, when's your first cross-country practice?" she asked.

"Um, I changed my mind. I don't think I'll go for the team."

"Did you lie to me?" She narrowed her eyes. "Were you

really trying to be Surge, like Alfie said?"

"No." I shook my head.

"That's good," she said. "That would be so lame. We're in grade six now."

I shrugged. "I'm just not sure I'm cut out for running."

"Forget about Surge," said Alfie the next day at recess.

"It was a terrible idea," I said.

Sam and Dylan were not playing soccer today. Instead they were talking to Shamini and Yoshie and Rachelle and Edebe. Edebe had just come to our school. She was from Lebanon. I wanted to join them, but my feet felt like they were glued to the dirt. So I watched as Dylan said something and Shamini threw her head back laughing.

"What could *he* say that was *soooo* funny?" I shook my head.

"Who knows," said Alfie.

Now Sam said something and Shamini laughed again. I could hear her squeal from where I was standing. "Why is she *squealing*?"

"Girls just do stuff like that," replied Alfie. "My sister and her friends squeal all the time. It's like living with a herd of seals."

I couldn't take my eyes off what was happening. Shamini was still laughing, her shoulders moving up and down.

Then beside me, Alfie blurted out, "Uh oh."

I turned and saw Adam and Carey coming toward us. A group of little kids scattered as they walked by. My body started shaking. I glanced around and couldn't see a teacher anywhere.

"Too late to run," said Alfie.

"I'm lousy at running anyway," I mumbled.

Adam and Carey headed right for me. I tried to step aside, but I wasn't quick enough and Adam hit his shoulder into mine. I stumbled a little. He didn't. He just laughed and kept walking. "What a lightweight," he said. "It's like you don't exist." He brushed his shoulder as if a fly had landed on it. My shoulder actually hurt from where he'd hit me.

After they'd strolled by, as if we were nothing, I unclenched my fists. "I wish I could just fight them off," I whispered.

"Yeah," said Alfie. "You're too small to fight *them*."

I had no reply. The truth hurt.

"BUT . . . what . . . if you were a ninja?!" Alfie smacked his forehead with his hand. "I've been thinking and thinking but that's it! Instead of Surge we need to train you as a ninja."

I remembered what Shamini had said about being in grade six now. I tried to scowl at Alfie. "Um, I don't think ninjas are cool anymore." Alfie and I had always played ninjas. Just thinking of them took me back to a time when I was okay, when people liked me. Or they put up with me. And we were all sort of the same size. Or if we weren't, it didn't matter.

"Of course they are," said Alfie. "They'll always be cool. They're ancient. This could be a good one for you. And they're small and sneaky and that's why they're so good at attacking their victims and getting away."

"We can't play ninjas on the playground," I said.

The excitement on Alfie's face disappeared. His shoulders sagged as he shoved his hands in his pockets. "Why can't recess be like before? We could play what we wanted instead of just standing around."

I kicked the ground with my foot.

"Maybe we should just play ninjas at your house," he said. "That would be okay."

"Yeah, okay," I said. In my backyard I didn't have to be in grade six.

CHAPTER EIGHT
THE NINJA CRAWL

After school, before we went to play in my back-yard, Alfie and I ate some nachos and cheese.

"Shamini told me that some guy won a hundred dollars at Bubba's for eating a hundred chicken wings," I said.

"Seriously? Wow." Alfie shoved nachos in his mouth. Then he snapped his fingers. "I think I read something where the money you win doubles on your birthday."

"Let's look it up," I said.

On my home computer (which was almost as ancient as my grandparents' TV), we googled Bubba's Restaurant. A picture of a guy with bulging muscles appeared on the screen. Bubba had been a WWE wrestler. He was kind of famous, at least in our town. He had some of the big, shiny belts he won for wrestling hanging in the restaurant. And lots of pictures with pop idols and movie stars.

"Look, here it is," said Alfie, pointing to the computer screen. "Under birthday deals. You could win two hundred dollars on your birthday. Oh, but you have to eat pizza too. One pizza and one hundred chicken wings to get the birthday double."

"That's impossible. I normally eat maximum ten wings. And I've never eaten a whole pizza."

"I have," said Alfie.

I started to see how Alfie had gotten so big over the summer.

I picked up the empty plate and took it to the sink. From the kitchen window, I glanced at Shamini's house. She wasn't home. I knew she was at soccer practice. I hoped she made the team. I really did. I wished I could talk to her about it, like we used to talk, on my front porch. But she was busy and I was scrawny.

Outside, Alfie showed me the ninja move he had looked up. I had to crawl on my hands and feet, keep my body straight and kind of walk like a crab.

"How about I time you," said Alfie.

"How about we time each other," I said. "You have to do this too." If I was going to look stupid, I wasn't doing it alone.

Alfie went first. I held his phone on the stopwatch app, and it took him thirty-one seconds to get from one end of our yard to the other. He stood up, panting and sweating. "That's so hard," he said.

"My turn," I said. I went to

the back of the yard and got into the position.

"Go," yelled Alfie.

I took off crawling. It was harder than I thought it would be. But I pushed myself. When I got to the end I stood up.

"Ho-ly," said Alfie. "Twenty seconds. You were a lot faster than me. I told you. This is something you can do, because you're little."

I shrugged. "What good does it do?"

"Makes you sneaky! So you can ambush your enemies."

I rolled on the ground, jumped up and got into a fighting position.

"See!!! You're going to be amazing."

"Let's forget about why we can use it," I said, "and see if we can bring our time down. For fun."

Alfie and I kept trying. Even if it didn't make us real ninjas, and even if it was lame, it *was* fun and gave us something to do outside. We figured out different ways of crawling and pretended we were fighting in a war.

And I found out I was good at being a ninja. Maybe being small and light wasn't so bad.

★ ★ ★

"I think we should practise your ninja crawl," said Alfie. We were doing nothing at recess but standing around. Again.

I was so sick of standing around, trying to look cool. Especially because, really, we weren't cool. "We have to go someplace where no one can see us." I glanced around the playground.

Dylan and Sam were playing basketball today. Shamini was playing soccer with some of her new grade seven friends. Only little kids were playing in the jungle gym area.

So far, all grade six meant was that Alfie and I were these in-between guys with nothing to do.

"And don't tell anyone what we're doing," I said. "No mention of ninjas to anyone. We're already labelled as losers because of that Surge thing."

"Gotcha." Alfie held up his thumb.

We made our way over to the emptiest area of the playground, far away from anyone else. We didn't need a lot of room, and we found the perfect spot under a tree.

"I was doing some research. If you get good at this you could enter this obstacle race thing. It's so in."

"I don't care about that," I said. It got me thinking. What did I care about? Why did I want to practise this? Was it because for once I felt like I was good at something? Or maybe I was just bored of being a boring grade sixer.

"Let's just do it for... something to do," I said.

Alfie nudged me. "Hey, it could give us

moves for the dance too. We can make that worm dance look supercool. Have you talked to Shamini about the dance yet?"

"I haven't had a chance," I said.

"I don't think I'll ask Naomi," said Alfie.

"Why not?"

"She hates me. I think that's a good enough reason."

"Let's forget about the dance," I said.

"Did you invite Shamini to Bubba's?"

I held up my thumb. "She's in."

"Does that mean you're getting a phone?"

"Hope so."

"Come on, recess will be over before we know it."

I was crawling on the ground, trying to get my knees up for better leverage, when I heard Alfie talking to someone. And I recognized the voices. Adam and Carey. Oh crap.

Before I could stand up, I heard the footsteps and felt the weight on my back.

"Nice chair," said Adam. He wiggled his butt into my back. It hurt.

I tried to hold myself up. But my arms collapsed and I fell to the ground. Adam laughed.

"Those twig arms aren't good for nothing." He walked away, and I stayed on the ground. Something felt mushy and gooey under me. And that something smelled really gross.

"Are you okay?" Alfie asked me.

"Are they gone?"

"Yes."

I sat up and looked around. They were gone. I looked down at my shirt. Oh no. Double gross! And my hands. Triple gross.

Dog poo!

CHAPTER NINE
GRADE SIX STINKS

The front of my shirt was covered in dog poo. My pants too. And my hands. The smell made me want to puke.

A soccer ball rolled over and Shamini ran toward us. She picked up the ball and put it under her arm just as the bell rang. "I'll walk in with you," she said. Then she put her nose in the air. "What is that smell?"

"Something really stinks," exclaimed Alfie.

What was I going to do? I couldn't go to class covered in dog poo. I sat still on the ground. I couldn't move.

"We better go," said Shamini.

So I stood.

Alfie and Shamini both looked at me. Then Alfie scrunched up his face. "Is that dog poo all over you?" He starting laughing and pinched his nostrils.

"You should change into your gym clothes," said Shamini.

"My mom is washing them," I moaned.

"Ask Mrs. Golden if you can go home and change," said Alfie. He grimaced. "It's not even poo," said Alfie. "It's doggy diarrhea!" Then he started laughing and slapping his legs.

"Be quiet," I said.

The side of Shamini's mouth twitched and I knew she was trying not to laugh. I avoided everyone as I headed into the school, but I could hear everyone asking about the smell. There was no way I could walk into the classroom. Alfie got Mrs. Golden for me.

"Can I go home and change?" I asked when she came out in the hall to see me.

She waved her hand in front of her face. "Whew. That is a little nasty. But I'm sure there will be something you can wear in the lost and found box. Or one of your friends will have something you can wear."

"Okay," I mumbled. This was a disaster.

"Archie," she said, in a kind voice, "this really is just a little mishap."

She told me there was a box of discarded clothing just outside the office. Thankfully, I made it down the hall without running into anyone. I rifled through the clothes and found dresses, a skirt that looked like it belonged to a grade one kid and some basketball muscle shirts. I didn't want to wear something with no arms, but my only other option was an extra-small Franklin the Turtle shirt. I found a pair of shorts and pulled them out. My stick legs would show. But at least they were boy shorts, and might fit.

I wanted to go home.

As I was going into the boys' washroom, Sam came out.

"Hey, Doggy Diarrhea." He put his arm up to cover his nose. "You stink, man."

I pushed by him and went into the washroom. When I saw myself in the mirror I groaned. The front of me was covered in a sloppy, brown, stinking mess. So disgusting! I whipped off the shirt and threw it in the trash can. No way was I taking it home to be washed. Then I saw my skinny body in the small mirror. I put on the muscle shirt. It looked horrible. It must have belonged to someone in grade eight. The armpits were almost down to my waist. I didn't want to wear the shorts either. The front of my pants weren't covered too badly, so I took them off and tried to wash them under the tap.

I was standing in my underwear, wearing a muscle shirt when I heard a rap on the door.

"Archie." It was Shamini.

I quickly put on my wet pants and opened the door a crack.

"Are you okay in there?" She sounded like my old friend again.

"Not really."

"I had a clean t-shirt in my bag." She handed it to me. "You can wear it."

I opened the door wider and took the folded shirt. It was PINK — and not just in colour. It had *PINK* in big letters across the front. "Thanks," I said, "but I've got this."

She stared at me. "Um, don't take this the wrong way. But that shirt is kinda too big. And you look like you peed yourself."

I glanced down at my pants. And that is exactly what the water stains looked like. Plus there were still some brown spots. Plus, I knew she was right about the shirt. I could feel air actually flowing through the vents of the giant armholes, which also gave a sneak peek of my skinny torso.

"At least mine will fit, and it's clean." She tried to smile.

Her t-shirt did smell clean. "I've got some shorts," I said.

"Put them on. Let me see what they look like. I'll wait outside the door. But hurry. You know Mrs. Golden, she's got a watch ticking in her brain."

I closed the door and whipped on the shorts and the shirt. Then I reopened the door.

"The shorts look okay. So does the shirt. Pink is in for guys you know."

"Thanks," I said. The shorts hung below my knees. And now I wore a neon pink shirt that literally screamed that it was pink.

Everyone would know I was wearing a girl's shirt. But was it worse that it was Shamini's?

"Um, thanks," I said.

"I gotta get back."

"Okay. You go. I'll just return these clothes to the lost and found."

I put the clothes in the box and walked like a turtle back to class. It took me a while to get up my nerve to go back. I stood outside the door for a few minutes, sucking in air, trying to breathe. Finally, I made my way in. I slunk my way back to my desk, hoping no one would notice me.

"Oh, look, it's Doggy Diarrhea," said Dylan. He laughed like a hyena.

Sam laughed too. Shamini tried not to laugh. Alfie laughed from the front of the class. I imagined a ninja crawling over to his desk and ambushing him.

"That's enough, people," said Mrs. Golden. "Accidents can happen to anyone. The next person I hear laughing will have to go clean up the schoolyard so that this doesn't happen again."

That sure shut everyone up.

Maybe I liked her more than I thought I did.

CHAPTER TEN
DO THE MATH

Monday morning, I got up and looked outside. Another sunny day in grade six. Too bad I didn't feel very sunny.

I stared at myself in the mirror. I had stick legs. And stick arms. And a stick chest. I was pathetic. There had to be something I could do. From my closet I took my baggiest jeans and a flannel button-down shirt. Flannel was thick material. Hot, but thick. I would have to suck up the hotness for the sake of looking bigger. Flannel would help me bulk up. I'd done the math. I was small. Clothes would help.

I walked over to Shamini's and knocked on her front door. Her mother opened it and smiled at me. "Archie, I haven't seen you for a long time."

"School's keeping me busy."

"Shamini's gone already, hon. She had an early soccer run." Then she smiled at me. "I heard it's your birthday tomorrow. Happy birthday!"

"Thanks," I said.

I walked back home and sat on the front porch to wait for Alfie. And I waited and waited. Where was he? Time ticked by. If I had a phone, I could text him. But my birthday wasn't until tomorrow. I was pretty sure I was getting a phone.

Suddenly, I knew I was going to be late. I ran to school. By the time I got there, I was sweating like I'd run the track a million times.

"Nice of you to join us, Archie," said Mrs. Golden when I tried to sneak into the classroom. "Next time you're late you will need a late slip."

I slid into my seat. Shamini glanced quickly at me and gave me a little wave.

Once Mrs. Golden's back was to the board, Dylan turned around.

"What's with the lumberjack shirt?" he asked. Then he laughed.

"You're sweating like a stuffed pig," he whispered. Of course, Mrs. Golden didn't hear him. She never heard *him*, only me.

I stared ahead so I wouldn't do something that would send me out in the hall. Out of the corner of my eye, I saw Dylan steal Shamini's pencil. I thought she would have a fit. But she just giggled.

Shamini poked Dylan. "Give it back," she whispered.

He turned and grinned at her. Then he stuck it in his mouth like he was a dog and it was a bone.

Shamini giggled *again*.

"Gross," she whispered.

Dylan took it out of his mouth and wiped it on his t-shirt. Then he gave it back to her. Seriously gross. On his shirt? But Shamini didn't seem to mind.

Now that she had her pen back, she was writing furiously, her hair falling in front of her face. Today she was wearing a purple t-shirt. It was kind of tight. Like painted on her body. I could see the outline of that new bra of hers. She was the only girl in the class to wear one.

I felt something hit me on the head. I looked down and saw a wadded up piece of paper. "What are you staring at?" Dylan smirked at me. "You look like you got puppy-dog-eyes."

I stopped staring at *what I was staring at* and glared at Dylan. "Nothing," I said.

"Okay, puppy-dog-eyes." He laughed. Then he whispered, "Hey, Shamini. Guess who's —"

Oh no! I didn't want him to tell Shamini anything. "I gotta a joke for you," I interrupted him. Shamini looked at me. I had to say it quickly to keep her attention on me and not Dylan. *Think. Think.* The only one I could remember was one Alfie had told me. When we were in grade one! "How do you make a tissue dance?" I blurted it out and waited only a second. "Put a boogey in it!" I laughed out loud.

"That's something a kindergarten kid would say," said Shamini. She shook her head at me.

"Juvenile," whispered Dylan before he turned around and stared ahead.

"Excuse me!" Mrs. Golden called out from the front. She had stopped writing on the board. "Mr. Zheng, would you like to share a joke with the rest of the class?"

I slid in my seat.

"I didn't think so."

I turned to the page Mrs. Golden had written on the board. It was hard to think, because I was boiling in my flannel shirt. Mrs. Golden droned on about concave and convex. Okay, at least I liked math a little. For homework we were supposed to look around our world and come up with things that looked concave (sunken in) or convex (pressed out). That was easy enough.

Mrs. Golden turned her back again. This time Dylan took Shamini's eraser. He stood up and tossed it in the air, catching it behind his back. Then he quickly slid into his seat.

"Tricky," she said. "Now give it back."

Tricky. Anyone could do that. Without thinking, I quickly reached over and grabbed Shamini's eraser out of Dylan's hand. I stood up and tried to throw it between my legs so I could catch it behind my back. I saw a kid with a hackey sack do it once, and it would be trickier than Dylan's trick. But my baggy pant leg was in the way. The eraser bounced off it and went flying in the air. When it came down, it hit Shamini in the eye.

"Oww." She put her hand to her eye.

"Sorry," I said, sheepishly.

"Did you throw an eraser at my face? Why would you do that, Archie?"

"Archie," called out Mrs. Golden. "I would prefer if you saved those moves for the schoolyard."

I sat down and lowered my head.

"Keep at your work, class," said Mrs. Golden, walking toward the door. "I will be right back. I expect proper behaviour." She glared at me over her glasses before she left. I buried my head in my books.

Out of the corner of my eye I saw Dylan steal Shamini's pen. Again. The guy had no imagination.

Dylan waved Shamini's pen in the air. Laughing, she tried to reach for it. Why was it okay for Dylan to do stupid stuff and not me? Shamini kept laughing and batting at her pen and Dylan kept pulling it back so she couldn't get it. It was all I could do not to stand up and grab it and give it back to her.

Hey, what if I did do that? I could be like a hero. I could be the one who got the pen back for the girl. And maybe it would stop her from being mad that I hit her in the face with her eraser. I leapt out of my seat and lunged toward the pen.

But my shirt got caught on the side of the desk.

How, I don't know. But it did. It pulled me back. My body pulled me forward. Then I heard the *rip*. And the *pops*.

Pop! Pop! Pop! Buttons flew everywhere. Suddenly, I was standing in the aisle with a wide open shirt. And no t-shirt underneath.

Dylan burst out laughing. Everyone else in the class joined him. The laughter went on and on, until it was high pitched and almost hysterical.

Then Dylan said, "Archibald has a concave chest! He just did our math homework for us!"

CHAPTER ELEVEN
BIRTHDAY BUCKS

"Happy Birthday!" My mother gave me a kiss and my father patted me on the back.

One of those gift bags my family reused over and over sat on the table. I eyed it.

"Thanks," I said. "I'm officially eleven."

"Open your gift," said my dad.

I picked up the bag and tore into it. I pulled out a box that looked like it had been used, like the bag. But it had a phone inside. The phone itself had a few scratches.

"It's second hand," said my dad. "But it still works great. I got it for a great deal off a guy from work."

I stared at it. "Do I have a plan?"

"Of course." said my father. He pointed to the box. "Here's your number." Then he went on to explain my plan, my limited text messages and limited data and limited everything.

"Don't abuse this privilege," said my mother. "You must always answer my text messages. And don't take it to school.

"I won't," I said.

But of course I did take it to school. I had to. I had to show Alfie and Shamini and put their numbers in. And anyone else who wanted to give me their number. Not that many kids had a phone so I was almost popular for a second until everyone realized my new phone was actually old. But Dylan didn't have one and that made me secretly happy.

All day at school, I thought of my birthday dinner. We talked about it at lunch. Shamini seemed excited. Maybe she got over my hitting her in the face with her own eraser the day before.

When it was time to head out to Bubba's Restaurant, I dressed in my nicest shirt and a pair of khaki pants. I even wore what my mom calls "real shoes" instead of sneakers. I went downstairs and my mother nodded her head in approval.

"Very nice, Archie." Then she walked over and fixed my collar. "You smell good too."

"Did you put on some of Dad's body spray?" Marvin made like the guy in the Axe commercial and pretended to spray his armpits. He also made hissing noises.

"No," I said quickly.

"Let's go," said my father.

"We have to wait for Shamini," I said.

"Oh, I told her just to watch for us," said my mother.

We went outside and, sure enough, Shamini came out her front door. I stared at her. She looked so pretty, so . . . like a girl. And so tall. I glanced down at her feet and noticed she was wearing some sort of shoe with a heel. She had on a bluey-greeny dress and her hair was pulled back. It even looked like she might have some shiny stuff on her lips. Like lipstick that my mother wore but shiny. Vaseline? ChapStick? No, it was pink. Her lips were the colour of cotton candy. It made her brown skin glow. And it made her look older. The shoes made her look taller. And the dress made her look like a model or something. I wasn't sure I wanted Shamini to look any older or better or taller or like a model. The only thing about the way Shamini looked that didn't make me a bit nervous was the birthday gift bag in her hand.

"Archie's the shortest," said Marvin as we climbed into our old car. "He should sit in the middle."

"I'll sit in the middle," said Shamini.

I liked sitting beside Shamini because she

smelled like dessert, like vanilla or cinnamon or something. I wondered if she could smell the body spray on me. (Yes, I had snuck some.) When we got to the restaurant, Alfie was waiting in the lobby, reading the menu. He also had a birthday gift bag, but he was dressed in some crazy cape and a big belt.

"Nice clothes," I said.

"It's exactly what Bubba wore when he was a wrestler. Except I didn't wear the skin tight shorts."

"Good thing," I said.

"I looked it up online and found the cape and belt at a costume store. I might wear it for Halloween." He swished the cape.

"I'm going to let you three sit at one table," said my mother. She kind of gave her head a little shake as she stared at Alfie and his get up. She liked Alfie but sometimes he was a bit over the top for her. "We will sit at another table."

"What about me?" Marvin whined.

"He can sit with us," said Shamini. She put her arm on Marvin's shoulder. Shamini had always been nice to Marvin, which was sometimes okay and sometimes annoying, like right now.

The host, who was also dressed in a sort of wrestling outfit, walked us to our table. "So who's the birthday boy?" he asked. His cape was smaller than Alfie's and just fit over his shoulders. All the staff wore the same t-shirts, and they had the belt as a kind of logo.

"Me," I said.

"You eat a hundred wings and you can win a hundred bucks. And be put on our wall." He pointed to a wall that had headshots of people with sauce all over their faces. Some were smiling. Most weren't.

Alfie leaned into me and whispered. "You should at least try. A hundred bucks is a lot."

"Your server will be with you in a minute," said the host before he left.

We sat down and I stared down at the menu, which doubled as a place mat. "What kind of wings do you like?" I asked my friends. "I'm hot all the way," said Alfie.

"Me too," said Shamini. "The hotter, the better."

"Me three," said Marvin.

I wasn't really a fan of hot food (neither was Marvin, but he was showing off). But I was with friends, and that's what they wanted.

"Go for the hundred," whispered Alfie. "The protein will help you grow. And the money will help you be rich."

"Let's see your new phone again," said Shamini.

I pulled it out. "I only have a few numbers on it so far. Like both of you and my parents. And I downloaded the Snapchat app, but my parents don't know it yet."

"They have Wi-Fi in here," said Alfie. "Let's look up wrestlers. I'll show you Bubba."

"I wonder if anyone has signed up for Mrs. Golden's wrestling team?" Shamini asked.

"Probably not," said Alfie. "It's not WWE."

We played around with all our phones and even took some selfies until our server came with water. "So what is everyone going to have?" she asked. "Everything is all-you-can-eat, so just let me know when you want more."

"Hot wings for all of us," I said.

"And pizza," said Alfie.

"Mom said one or the other," said Marvin. "Since you got a phone."

"Shhh," I said. "It's my birthday party. He can have pizza."

"So you're the birthday boy! If you eat a hundred wings you can win a hundred bucks," said the server. "Add a large pizza to that and it's two hundred bucks."

"Oh man," said Alfie. "I wish it was my birthday. I'm definitely coming here for my party."

We all ordered wings and a large pizza for the table.

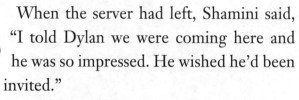

When the server had left, Shamini said, "I told Dylan we were coming here and he was so impressed. He wished he'd been invited."

Dylan wished he'd been invited to my party? Or did he just want to be with Shamini?

"Let's go look at the wall while we're waiting for our food," said Alfie.

We slid out of our booth seats and went over to huge bulletin board. As we scanned the pictures I saw no one I knew until . . . there was a face I knew. I swear my eyes bugged out of my head. "Look!!" I pointed at the face.

"Oh man, it's Adam!" Alfie slapped his forehead. "We can't get away from that guy."

"I can't believe he ate that many wings," said Shamini.

Alfie stared at me. Then he mouthed. "You have to do this!"

CHAPTER TWELVE
WING DING

The server, her cape flowing behind her, reappeared just as we slid back into the booth. She had a tray of big plastic glasses. Everyone had ordered Coke.

"All drinks are refillable too," she said putting them on the table. "I'll be right back with your wings and pizza."

When the server came back the next time, she had little red plastic baskets full of wings. And a pepperoni pizza.

"How do you know how many he eats?" Archie asked her.

"We keep track by baskets.

There are ten to a basket."

"I would have to eat ten of these?" I pointed to the basket the server had placed in front of me.

"That's it. Good luck."

When the server left our table, Shamini looked at me. "You're not really thinking of doing this. Are you?"

I shrugged. I thought about Dylan and how he kept stealing her pencil and how she seemed to like that. Was she impressed that I might try to do this?

"I think so," I said, trying to act like someone cooler than I was.

"You're crazy."

The first ten wings went down pretty good. The heat of the wings burned a little in my throat and my stomach, but they weren't *that* bad. So I called the server over and ordered another basket.

"How does he know I'm not eating them for you?" Alfie whispered.

"I heard that," said the server. She pointed up at the ceiling. "Cameras."

"Oh," said Alfie. "Hi tech."

"Bubba thought of everything."

The second basket went down pretty good too! I wasn't stuffed. So I ordered a third.

"You're going to blow up," said Shamini.

"Nah. I'm a growing boy," I said.

"And soon to be a rich growing boy," said Alfie. "When you're done we'll make sure your photo is right beside Adam's. You can take a selfie with your photo and we can spread it around social media. Maybe Adam will be impressed and stop bugging us."

I kept eating. And eating and eating. Three baskets turned into four, then five, then six. At six I needed a break. My stomach was starting to hurt. And now my mouth burned from the hot sauce. I was also starting to sweat. I leaned back in my seat.

"Drink water, it will help," said Alfie. "And keep your eye on the prize."

"You don't have to do this," said Shamini. "It's kind of a silly thing to do."

Dylan stealing her pencil flashed in my mind. Lately, Shamini seemed to like silly. And then I saw Adam in my mind too. What would Adam think when he saw my picture next to his? "I'm okay," I said. "I can do it."

So I drank some water. But it didn't make me feel better. Not even a little bit. In fact it made me feel worse. It felt like the chicken was floating around in big pool in my stomach.

The waiter dropped off another basket. I looked at it, and the wings seemed to be flapping.

"Four more," said Alfie.

"Don't do it," said Shamini.

I had to do it. I chewed. And swallowed. Shamini looked at me and shook her head. I took another wing. And chewed. And swallowed.

"You can do it," said Alfie, sounding like a coach. "Come on. I know you got it in you."

I kept going. One wing at a time. My cheeks filled like a chipmunk's then I forced myself to swallow the chewed meat. I ate wing after wing until I had finished another basket.

"Three to go." Suddenly, I was feeling very weird. The sight of the chewed bones made me want to gag.

"Ho-ly," said Alfie. "You're down to the wire."

Alfie was clearly impressed. Was I impressing Shamini as much as Alfie? I tried to sit tall and pretend I was a hero or something. But I had a bad feeling in my stomach. At first I thought it was because I needed to burp, which of course I couldn't do at the table. But then it started to feel like the chicken was floating higher and higher and moving from my stomach to my throat. Hot sauce burned my throat. I tried to breathe and push it all back down. But it was like a pool that was overflowing. Up and over. Only mine would be out and over.

"Excuse me," I mumbled.

I got up and walked quickly away from our

table. When I felt the food getting closer and closer to my mouth I ran. The first washroom was the handicapped one. I pushed open the door. But I didn't make it to the toilet. I puked all over the washroom floor. It was gross. It was disgusting and smelly. Before I grabbed a handful of paper towels and got down to clean it all up, I locked the door. No one — and I mean no one — could see me like this.

Ewwwww. Big chunks of chicken. I gagged at the smell. Everywhere I looked there was a piece of chicken. Gross! But I did my best. Soon, the small trash can started overflowing with paper towels.

Finally, I had it all cleaned up, or as best as I could do. Then I stood up and stared at myself in the mirror. Orange splotches had landed on my good shirt and some was in my hair. I tried to clean off my shirt with more paper towels. Then I turned on the tap and stuck my head under the water. Hoping that I'd rinsed most of it out, I shook my head like a dog after it had a bath.

Someone knocked on the door. "Archie?"

It was Marvin. "Be out in a minute," I said.

"I looked everywhere for you. Why are you in the handicapped restroom? You're not supposed to be in there. What are you doing in there?"

"None of your business," I said.

"They're paying the bill. Mom sent me to check on you but I couldn't find you. Alfie's dad is here to take him home."

I flushed the toilet one more time then opened the door.

He looked at me and laughed like a hyena. "You barfed."

"I did not." I stormed away from him to the restaurant lobby. I saw my mom and dad, but no Shamini or Alfie. My mother was holding my gift bags.

"Where's Shamini and Alfie?" I asked.

"You were gone for a long time," said my mother. "Alfie's father came to get him, so Shamini got a ride with him. They both said you were sick."

I felt even sicker. I wrecked my birthday dinner by eating too much. What a loser.

"Let's get out of here," I said. The fresh air outside felt really good. I sucked in a big breath. And exhaled. My stomach was starting to feel better. Maybe because it had nothing in it now.

When we got in the car, I slouched down and stared out the window. We had just gotten out of the parking lot when my mother turned around.

"Why did you eat so much?" she asked.

"The wings were *free* because it was my *birthday*."

"You didn't win the hundred bucks," said Marvin.

No, I didn't. And I embarrassed myself. Again.

CHAPTER THIRTEEN
DOLLAR STORE

The next morning I didn't want to go to school. How was I going to face Shamini? I wondered if I could convince my mom I was sick. Then I could actually have a reason for last night's disaster.

My mother called from the bottom of the stairs, telling me to get a move on. I made my way to the bathroom I shared with Marvin. Shirtless and only wearing boxers, Marvin shook his head at me and laughed.

"What?" I snapped.

"You are so skinny. I can see your ribs."

I pushed by him and slammed the bathroom

door. This time I totally avoided looking at myself. What was there to look at? A skinny kid, almost the smallest in grade six. Who puked up his own birthday dinner.

At least it was cool and cloudy out. I could legit wear baggy clothes and not look like I was trying to hide my body. Alfie showed up on time for once and we decided to ride our bikes.

We got to school just as the bell rang. I was happy that we didn't have to hang around outside. Shamini glanced at me when I sat down in class and I gave her a little wave. She gave me a little wave back.

"How are you feeling?" She whispered.

"I think I had the flu," I said sheepishly. Mrs. Golden had her back to the class, busy writing something on the board. "Um, thanks for the movie passes."

Shamini had gotten me movie passes so I could go see *Jimmy Bond*.

Finally. I was probably the only kid in the class who hadn't seen it yet. Alfie got me a certificate to go buy a video game at the best gaming store. It had the best selection and all the latest games.

Dylan turned around. "I heard you wimped out on the wings at Bubba's," he whispered.

My stomach suddenly felt sick again. And it wasn't because I had eaten too many wings. Why would Shamini tell *him*?

By the time school ended for the day it had turned rainy. Playing ninjas in my backyard would be too messy, so Alfie and I watched TV. But we were bored.

"I wish I had a life like Jimmy Bond," groaned Alfie. "A billionaire who rides on yachts and motorcycles and everything he owns is cool and has, like, hidden devices. The guy has, like, unlimited money."

"I wish I could go to the video store with the gift certificate you gave me and get a new game," I said. "Then we wouldn't be bored."

"Hey, I've got an idea. Why don't we walk to the dollar store?" Alfie pulled a ten dollar bill from his pocket. "And buy things that might be like Jimmy Bond's gadgets. Could be fun. Give us something to dream about."

"Where'd you get that?" I pointed to the money.

"I told a lie for my sister about who she was out with. She owed me. Big time. Plus, she made me leave a bedroom window open so she could come in late. Twice!" He held up two fingers. "It's a good job."

"It's not a job," I said.

"Is to me. So, you wanna go to the dollar store?"

"Sure," I said. There was nothing else to do and my mother wasn't home. She'd left us alone to go to the grocery store and I'd already had three text messages. Some freedom.

Marvin was at a friend's house. "We can take umbrellas."

"Let's ride our bikes. Quicker," said Alfie.

I texted my mother to tell her what I was doing (she would take my phone away if I didn't), then we got on our bikes and braved the rain pellets crashing down from the sky. After shaking the water out of our hair, we walked in the store. The man at the checkout eyed us like he thought maybe we didn't have money. That was usually the case. Sometimes Alfie and I came to this store and never bought anything.

I went straight to the toy weapons. "Look at this sword," I said.

Alfie picked up one too. Then we started sword fighting. The man behind the cash left his post and came to our aisle. "You break, you buy."

"Why don't we get these?" Alfie held up two long skinny pens that were also flashlights. "We can take them to school and have fun in class pointing them at kids. We could pretend they're laser beams that can make a person faint. Or start barking like a dog." He started howling and the man came and glared at us again.

"We're getting these," said Alfie to the man.

"You sure?" I asked. It was his money.

"You shoulda won the hundred dollars. We could have bought a hundred things in here." Alfie stared at the price tag. "Why do they call it a dollar store when these are two dollars? Makes no sense." He shrugged.

"Why would Shamini tell Dylan I puked?"

"She's kind of turned into the most popular girl at school. Those kinds of girls tell everything. Do you know if she's going to the dance with him?"

"I dunno," I said. "She always said she would go with me."

"You better ask her before he does. Just saying."

"And you better ask Naomi." I glared at Alfie.

"I don't care if I go with

Naomi. You care if you go with Shamini. Different stories." He picked up another pen. "I'll buy an extra pen and you can give it to Shamini. She'll like that."

We picked out the three best pens. I even got one with shiny pink jewels on it for Shamini.

"They're called rhinestones," said Alfie. "My sister got mad at me 'cause she thought I took her rhinestone earrings."

"Did you?"

"Yeah."

Alfie paid for the pens. Even after tax Alfie had some change, so I didn't feel that bad that we'd spent all *his* money. Not my money. His money. We rode our bikes back to my place in the crazy rain. When we got there we had water all up our backs.

"I'm thinking I should just ride home," said Alfie. "I need to change into dry clothes. And you don't have one single thing that would fit me."

"Yeah, okay," I said. My mother was home now and she would make us put our clothes in the dryer. So Alfie would sit around my room in his underwear. Gross.

"But don't forget," I said. "Bring the pens to school."

CHAPTER FOURTEEN
NONE OF YOUR BUSINESS

The next day the schoolyard was dotted with puddles, but the sun was shining. Mrs. Golden talked about her wrestling team again. No one put up their hand to join.

All morning I watched Dylan turn around to talk to Shamini. I wondered if Shamini was going to go to the dance with him. I wanted to give her the pen, but I never had the chance.

Finally, the bell went and I stood up. I wanted to walk out with Shamini, but Naomi called her over. I could see Alfie was right. Shamini was definitely the most popular girl in the class. She had four other girls surrounding her.

Alfie caught up with me and said, "Did Shamini like her pen?"

"I haven't given it to her yet."

"Oh. Okay. We can give it to her on the schoolyard. If she's not playing soccer."

Once again, we were just standing around when I saw Shamini come out. She didn't have a soccer ball with her or her gym clothes on. And she was only with Naomi.

I nudged Alfie. "Let's go over to the girls now."

But Alfie was busy pointing his pen at something. "It would be so cool to actually have a pen that shot laser beams," he said. "Or snake venom!"

I pulled my cell phone out of my pocket. "Or a phone that did something cool too. Hey, maybe I should text Shamini. You think she'd answer?"

Alfie shrugged. "Not supposed to at school, but she might."

Then I heard the voice behind me. "Ohhhh what's the little loser got?"

"Not again," said Alfie. He spun around and pointed the pen in Adam's eyes. "Take that," he said.

Adam laughed. I saw Carey coming over too. I froze. Like a brick of ice. Like I'd been zapped by Mr. Icicle.

Alfie tugged my shirt. "Come on! Let's go."

I sucked in a breath and started running. But I hadn't gone even two steps before I felt Adam's hand on my hoodie. I spun around. Alfie hadn't gotten very far either. Carey was holding the back of his shirt.

Carey grabbed Alfie's pen out of his hand. "What is this? A *magic* pen?"

"Give it back," said Alfie. He tried to grab it, but Carey waved it in high the air. Even too high for Alfie. "Awwww, he wants his pen back."

Suddenly, Adam lunged at me. He tried to grab my phone, but I held on tight. Adam started flinging me around, but I wouldn't let go. I was like a dog with a bone. Adam flung me so hard we both tumbled to the ground, splashing in a mud puddle.

And just like that a teacher loomed over us. It was, of course, Mrs. Golden.

"What's going on here?"

I couldn't speak.

"Carey took my pen," said Alfie.

"Please, get up," she said to Adam and me.

She held out her hand. "Hand over the phone." I stood up, gave her my phone and hung my head.

"All four of you are going to the office," said Mrs. Golden.

I'd never been sent to the office. She waved to another teacher and called out, "Take over for me. I'm taking these boys to the office."

"Why do I have to go to the office?" Alfie asked as he walked beside Mrs. Golden. His hair bobbed up and down.

"Obviously, you didn't listen to my rules."

Mrs. Golden kept Adam and Carey ahead of her, probably to keep them from running away on her. She walked fast and Alfie puffed beside her. I walked on her other side and thought about her rules. Thing was, she was right. I hadn't listened and Alfie probably hadn't either.

"What rule?" Alfie asked.

"There is a rule that says zero tolerance for fighting in the schoolyard."

"Oh," said Alfie. "But we didn't start it."

The entire schoolyard stared at us as Mrs. Golden marched us into the school. What was going to happen? Would they suspend me? Take away my phone for good? Call my mother at work? I wanted to go directly to the washroom to throw up. I was good at puking.

At the office, Alfie and I got a lecture from

Principal Fujimoto about the zero tolerance rule, and then we were told to get back to class.

"Um, what about my phone?" I asked.

"Come see me after final bell."

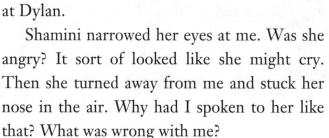

Back in class, I slithered into my seat. Shamini caught my eye and mouthed, "What happened?"

"None of your business," I snapped. "If I tell you you'll just blab to him." I pointed at Dylan.

Shamini narrowed her eyes at me. Was she angry? It sort of looked like she might cry. Then she turned away from me and stuck her nose in the air. Why had I spoken to her like that? What was wrong with me?

After school I had to wait to get my phone from the office, so I walked home alone. My mother was there to greet me at the door when I got home. "What were you thinking, Archibald, taking your phone to school?"

My shoulders slumped.

"I told you to be responsible with it." She used her hands to talk. "You're very lucky Mrs. Golden is nice."

"She's not that nice." I walked into the kitchen.

My mother followed on my heels. "You need to follow the rules."

"Okay. Okay." I knew I was being grumpy. But Shamini hadn't said another word to me all day. And it was my fault. I'd snapped at her when she was just caring what happened to me.

"You're acting very funny lately. Is something wrong? Are you not doing well with your marks?"

"My marks are good."

"That's what Mrs. Golden said too. She also said she wants you to join her wrestling team."

"What?!" I turned and stared at her.

She put her hands on her hips. "So I told her you would."

"You *said* you didn't want me in extra things." Now I used my hands to talk, like huge gestures. "And that we don't have money and Dad doesn't want to drive me around all weekend after working all week."

"This wrestling team doesn't cost any money. And she said she would drive you to all the meets if I gave her permission, so I did."

"Mom, noooooooo!"

CHAPTER FIFTEEN

TO LIBERATE OR . . .

"What am I going to do?" I groaned. I flopped on the sofa. "I don't want to be the only one having wrestling practice and driving around with Mrs. Golden. And me, wrestling? I'm going to get killed."

"Let's play the *Liberator* video game," said Alfie. "Right now he's the best wrestler in the world. He's unbelievable. Get your mind off your predicament. And believe me, you are in a predicament."

"I have to go to my first practice Monday. I don't want to go."

Alfie put in the video game and we both took our spots with our controllers. Maybe a video game about a wrestler would take my mind off the school wrestling team and, oh, the grade six dance. I was sure Shamini wouldn't want to go with me now.

The Liberator flashed on the screen to introduce his video game. He was huge, muscles bulging everywhere. And he had a ton of tattoos. He had blond hair that he wore in a ponytail, and he always wore a headband. My grandpa said he reminded him of some old wrestler named Hulk Hogan or this other guy named Bret Hart. He said Bubba wasn't all that great, but that the Liberator was smart and strong. I'd spent a lot of time watching his fights this summer. Today, though, I didn't have the energy to play a video game. All my energy had been spent being a loser at school.

We had played for around ten minutes before Alfie threw his remote down and jumped up from his spot on the sofa.

"That's it! I've got it!"

"Got what?" I asked. I didn't even look at him.

"You have to be like the Liberator. That's how you're going to grow and handle this wrestling stuff and not freeze when you are in trouble. And get Shamini to go to the dance with you. You need to bulk up. If you get strong, you might have confidence. You can be short but strong!"

"Bulk up?"

"Lift weights! We could go to the gym?"

"What gym?" I asked.

"At the community centre. There's a big weight room."

"I think you have to be fourteen to get in there," I said.

"We'll sneak in," said Alfie. "I'll go online and make up a program for us."

At least he'd said 'us.' Maybe what he said made *some* sense. Maybe I could get stronger. Maybe it could give me confidence. Maybe it could help both of us.

★ ★ ★

"I think it's wonderful you boys are going to the community centre today," said my mother. We were taking our swim trunks and towels so she would think we were swimming. What she really meant was — I'm so glad you're not playing video games all day. She dropped us off at the front doors and said, "I'll pick you up in two hours."

"Sure thing," I said.

"Thanks for the ride," said Alfie.

"Okay, so how do we do this?" I asked as we walked to the boys' change room.

"I've got a plan," said Alfie.

He didn't say anything more while we got changed, and headed out to the weight room. Inside my stomach was flip flopping. My hands were sweating too. And my throat was really dry. Why was I so nervous? Oh, because I was doing something I wasn't supposed to be doing. Again.

"There's a back door," said Alfie. "The big-wig supervisor always stands near the front by the desk. So all we have to do is get someone to let us in the back door. Then we can work out on the weights where the supervisor can't see us."

"So, it's locked is what you're saying?"

"Well, yeah. But someone will let us in."

I was right about the door being locked. We tried it just in case. No go. Now we had to see if Alfie was right about someone letting us in. Two people were working out close to the door. A buff guy, like a really buff guy, and a girl who looked fit. Strong. Stronger than me. In fact I was sure she could haul me down with one arm.

"Best bet is the guy," I said.

Alfie puffed up his chest, stood tall and tried to get his attention. But then the girl turned. First he waved at her but she didn't respond. Then he really waved, flapped his arms. This time she glared at us. Then he rapped on the glass.

"Maybe we should go swimming," I said. "We could lift weights in my basement."

"And how would we do that?"

"I don't know. I saw on YouTube where someone used paint cans."

"We need the real free weights and a bench. I did my research."

He rapped again. This time the girl shook her head at us. But she walked over to the door. Alfie made grand gestures to the door. As soon as she opened it, Alfie said, "My brother is in here. I have to get him."

She shrugged and rolled her eyes. "Whatever."

We both walked in and looked around. I leaned in to Alfie and whispered, "We can't work out around her now. She'll know we lied."

Alfie whispered back, "Let's go to that corner. We'll be hidden there."

We hurried over to the quiet corner at the back of the room. It was perfect.

"Okay, so stretch a bit and then lie on the bench," said Alfie. "The first exercise is bench press. It's for building up your chest muscles."

Alfie showed me a few stretches, and I knew a few of my own. I tried to look as if I knew what I was doing, but my stomach felt like I'd done way too many somersaults.

"Do you think we should be in here?" I whispered.

"Trust me," said Alfie.

CHAPTER SIXTEEN
PRESS IT

"Trust you," I said. "Now that's a problem."

"Lie down on the bench." Alfie spoke like he was a drill sergeant.

I figured I might as well try to do something, since we had managed to get in the weight room. I put my water bottle on the floor. Instead of water, it was filled with some fancy orange stuff that Alfie had given me so I wouldn't pass out. Smart thinking on Alfie's part. I lay down on my back and Alfie put some weights on a bar. Then he lifted it — which he could barely do. He handed the bar to me. By now my arms were stretched up. I was ready. This would be easy.

Just press it up and down and up and down as many times as I could.

The bar hit my hands. I dropped it on to my chest.

"Press it," said Alfie.

I tried. I really did. But the weight wouldn't budge off my chest. There was no way I could lift it.

"How much did you put on there?" I asked. "I can't move it."

"Try harder." Alfie's big face was right above me.

I breathed in, filling my cheeks with air, closed my eyes and pushed. I pushed until I thought my cheeks would pop and my brains would blast out of my head. Then I let out all the air I had in my mouth and made a huge grunting noise. I opened my eyes and stared at the ceiling. The weight still sat like a big rock on me. I was starting to feel trapped.

"You didn't even get it up a centimetre," said Alfie.

"Get it off of me," I muttered.

"Try again."

"No! Off. Now." This time I yelled.

"Okay. Okay. Shhhh." He put his finger to his mouth and looked around.

He was right, I shouldn't yell. But the weight was pressing on me and I wanted it off. I wanted to scream.

"We'll take some of the weight off and try again," he suggested.

"I'm not trying again," I said through clenched teeth.

"Okay, okay. First let's get it back on the rack. Then we'll talk."

Alfie grabbed the bar and the two of us tried to lift it. But it was hard. And awkward. I was breathing so hard I thought I was going to pass out. My throat was all clogged and dry. I kept pressing and using every ounce of strength I had. We were almost there when one of the weights on one side started slipping off.

"Oops," said Alfie. "I guess I didn't put it on properly."

The weight crashed to the mat and clanged against another weight. Boy, did it echo. I wanted to look around and see if anyone had heard. But with most of the weight still on top of my chest, that was almost impossible. The noise seemed really loud though.

"That's one way to solve the problem," said Alfie. "Sit up," he said. "It's lighter now."

I sat up, bringing the bar forward. But it was so lopsided I couldn't hang on to it. Another weight rolled off the end and onto the mat. This time it crashed against my water bottle. The top of the bottle flew off and syrupy orange drink spread all over the mat.

"Oops again," said Alfie.

"Are you boys supposed to be in here?" a stern voice said. A huge man, muscles popping out everywhere, loomed over us.

"It's okay," said Alfie. "We're just small for our age."

"What's going on over here?"

The weight room supervisor headed over. He looked official in his track suit and name tag.

"Uh, oh," said Alfie. "We'd better get out of here."

"Help me with this," I said.

Alfie and I managed to put the weight on the ground in a nanosecond. Funny, how you can get things done under *real* pressure. When you know you're in *real* trouble.

I picked up my water bottle, and saw the mess of flowing orange on the floor, which was turning to sticky orange. *Never mind*, I thought.

Alfie grabbed my shirt and said, "We gotta go!"

This time I didn't freeze. No, I didn't. I ran, jumping over a bench and not even falling. We bolted for the back door of the weight room. Alfie pushed open the door and we sprinted down the hall. I think I might have been running faster than I did on the track, if that was possible.

"We have to hide," said Alfie, huffing and puffing. "If he catches us we'll be banned. I have to bring my little brother swimming here tomorrow. How will . . . how will . . . I explain to my mother I can't take him? It's his birthday. He'll cry."

Alfie could hardly talk. And he was sweating. Sweat ran down his face like water out of a faucet.

We ran down the back hallway and out into the main lobby. And that's when we ran into Shamini! Like, seriously ran right into her.

How could my luck be so bad? Shamini was with Yoshie, Rachelle, Naomi and Edebe. They had beach bags slung over their shoulders.

"Archie?" Shamini frowned at me.

"Um, um, hi, Shamini." My voice shook. I know it sounded super high. I was panting like a dog in hot weather without water. Or actually, panting like a dog in hot weather with a dog catcher after him. Someone with a net.

"He's trying to be the Liberator," said Alfie. "But we can't talk now!" He pointed down the hallway where the supervisor rounded the corner and rushed toward us.

"Hey, you two," he called out.

"Why is he chasing you?" Naomi asked. "He doesn't look happy."

"Keep running, Archie," said Alfie.

"Gotta go, Shamini," I said. I turned, took two steps and bashed into a little table with notices and brochures on it.

"Ouch," I yelled. I sent the table clanging to the floor. The slippery brochures flew to the floor. They skidded all over the place, including somehow under my feet.

I landed with a thud among the brochures.

CHAPTER SEVENTEEN
SURPRISE!

"Run," yelled Alfie.

Unfortunately, my feet were up in the air, not on the floor. The face of the supervisor loomed above me. I couldn't even crawl away.

"You need to clean up your mess," said the supervisor.

As I stood up, Shamini whispered, "Archie, you are acting *so weird*."

The supervisor handed a wet rag to me and one to Alfie. Then he jerked his head toward the weight room.

"The orange was, um, not my idea," said Alfie. He leaned into me and whispered. "Sorry.

Don't want to rat you out, but it's my brother's birthday tomorrow."

Naomi stared at me for a second. "The Liberator. Is that true? That is hilarious. Weren't you also trying to be Surge?"

"I can't believe this," said Shamini. She was shaking her head and her cheeks were turning red. "I can't believe *you*!"

"He just wanted to be able to get big like the Liberator," Alfie said. He flexed but not many muscles popped.

I wanted to disappear. Be invisible. Yoshie had her hand to her mouth, but I could tell she was giggling. Rachelle and Naomi didn't even try to hide their giggles behind their hands. They laughed right out loud. Shamini looked at me with an expression I'd never seen on her face. I think it was shame.

"Seriously, the Liberator, Archie?" she said. "What grade are you in?"

"Guys," said the supervisor. "I really need you to clean up your mess."

"Let's go swimming," said Rachelle to Shamini. "And leave Sticklegs to grow muscle so he can be the Liberator." She giggled and so did Naomi. Edebe just stared at me.

Shamini didn't giggle either. "Don't call him *that*," she said.

I watched Shamini walk away and exhaled, like really loudly. Now she really thought I was weird. I turned around to stare at Alfie. "Why?" I asked him. "Why would you say anything about the Liberator? You made us look like geeks. Dweebs. Losers."

"It was the truth," he said.

"Come on you two, let's go back to the weight room," interrupted the supervisor.

The supervisor marched us back to the weight room, opened the door and ushered us inside. The big guy with the massive muscles smirked at us. "Welcome back boys." He gave us this funny wink. "Bit sticky back there."

We were down on our hands and knees scrubbing the rubber mat when Alfie said, "That was nice of her to stick up for you."

"Who?"

"Shamini. When Naomi called you Sticklegs she told her not to. Maybe she still likes you, a little anyway."

"I'm not listening to any more of your ideas."

"They're not *that* bad. They're just not working out."

I didn't have an answer to that.

"I'll think of something else." Alfie said.

"NO!" I stood up. "We're done. I'm done."

"Waste of a good drink," said Alfie.

"Let's get out of here," I said.

We handed in our rags and the supervisor checked out the job we did. We must have cleaned up okay, because he told us he wasn't going to ban us from using the community centre. Then he gave us the spiel about where we could go and where we couldn't go. "Sixteen to get in the weight room, boys."

Sixteen? We thought it was fourteen. We'd even messed that up.

We left the weight room, through the front door, and walked out into the main lobby.

"What should we do now?" I asked. "My mom's not coming for hours."

"We could swim," said Alfie. "We brought our trunks."

"Not a chance," I said. "I'm not going in there now."

"Oh right. The girls are swimming."

We walked by glass and I stared at my reflection. My legs were pretty skinny. Naomi had been right.

"We could eat," said Alfie.

"I don't have any money," I said.

"Neither do I," groaned Alfie. "My sister is grounded so I've been laid off."

"If no one is in the gym we could try basketball," I said.

"We'd suck," he said. He snapped his fingers. "Oh, but I just remembered that there's a room around here that has mats on the floor. If no one is in it, we could do somersaults and stuff. That'd be fun."

At this point I didn't care what I did. Shamini hated me. "Okay," I said, "but only if no one is in the room. If anyone comes in we can say we're practising wrestling."

Alfie held up his thumb. "Gotcha."

Alfie guided us down a few halls, passing by the gym. Yup, we would have been out of place in there. When we hit a sign that said Utility Room we entered. Empty.

We horsed around on the mats doing somersaults and dive rolls and pathetic flips. I kept thinking about Shamini and how she had said I was acting weird. I guess I wasn't sure how to act anymore. Not even with my best friends. Grade six was destroying me.

The exercise did take my mind off my sorry

life. I had worked up a sweat when I heard a familiar voice at the door. I turned to see Mrs. Golden come into the Utility Room.

"Hello, boys," said Mrs. Golden.

"What is she doing here?" Alfie whispered to me.

With Mrs. Golden was a man, I'm guessing her husband. He was around her height, so not tall. And not super thick either. But he looked fit. He looked fast and strong. He was kinda bald and wore wire-rimmed glasses.

"Boys, this is my husband, Mr. Golden."

"Hi boys," he said.

"Nice to meet you," I moved toward him and held out my hand like my father had taught me. He shook it, then he shook Alfie's hand.

"*You're* the wrestling guy?" Alfie had a huge grin on his face.

"I am," he said.

"We were practising wrestling. Archie is really into it."

With my mouth wide open, I stared at Alfie. We weren't really practising wresting. What was he talking about? We were just messing around.

Mrs. Golden looked at her husband. "These are the boys I was telling you about."

"Can you teach us some moves?" Alfie asked, before I could even say we had to leave.

I wanted to groan, but I kept all sounds to myself. Inside I think I might have been ready to boil over. It was bad enough that I had to go to practice on Monday. My mother said if I didn't go she'd take away my phone. And now wrestling was ruining my whole weekend.

I grudgingly followed Mr. and Mrs. Golden over to the mats.

"First we'll demonstrate," said Mrs. Golden.

Mr. Golden took off his glasses and carefully put them out of the way. Then Mrs. Golden stood across from Mr. Golden and they both squatted low and looked each other in the eye. They moved around a bit in a circle. Suddenly, like the snap of a finger, Mrs. Golden lunged and grabbed Mr. Golden. She lifted him up and dumped him on the ground. Then she pinned him. I think my jaw dropped to the ground next to Mr. Golden.

"Wow!" said Alfie. "You're good Mrs. Goldie. I mean Mrs. Golden."

"Don't worry," she said. "I know you kids call me Goldie-Oldie. But I bet you didn't know I could flip like that." She winked. "Some of us *old* gals can still move."

Mr. Golden stood up and looked at us. "First we will teach basic stances. But it won't be long before you will be flipping your opponent and pinning him with a half nelson."

"A half nelson?" Alfie sounded excited.

"Um, I will never be able to lift anyone," I said. "Everyone is bigger than me."

Mr. Golden put a hand on my shoulder. "You won't go against someone

like Alfie. You will compete in a lightweight category."

"Really? Lightweight? They have a category for that?"

"I started at your age and I was about your size. I won a lot of matches and I stayed lightweight my entire life."

"Do you think I could join too?" Alfie asked.

"Of course," said Mrs. Golden. "You'll be wonderful."

I don't think I'd ever seen Alfie so happy. And strange as it sounds, I was feeling better too.

CHAPTER EIGHTEEN

IT'S NOT OKAY

Alfie and I practised wrestling all day Sunday in my backyard. We went over and over the basic stances, trying to knock each other down. I was at a disadvantage for sure, but it had still been fun. I kept hoping Shamini would come over to watch us but she didn't. I'd sent her a text but she didn't answer me. I only sent one, because Alfie said sending any more would make me look like a loser.

As I was leaving my house Monday morning, I saw Shamini coming out of her house with her mother. I was about to go back in and pretend I had forgotten something but Shamini called out to me.

"Archie, can I talk to you for a sec?"

"Um, sure," I said. I heard her tell her mother to wait in the car for her.

I walked down my walk and met her on the sidewalk in front of our houses.

"I texted you," I said.

"I wanted to talk to you in person," she said. "Archie, something's going on with you. You've changed."

"Um, not really," I said. "I haven't grown even an inch."

"I'm not talking about size," she said. "Who cares about that? We used to be best friends."

Used to be? What was she saying?

Her mother honked the horn.

"I have to get going," she said. "I have a dentist check-up." She started walking toward the car, but turned around to say, "I don't like the way you're changing. That's what I wanted to say to you."

I watched her walk away. My heart sank. Had I just lost my best friend? I walked to school by myself, going over every word she had said.

Shamini didn't show up for school before the recess bell. And I was late getting out for recess because I had to talk to Mrs. Golden about a math question. Alfie was waiting for me. I saw Shamini with Naomi and Edebe. Her mother must have just dropped her off.

I stood still for a second and stared at her. I was afraid to do anything. Last year I would have just gone up to her and we would have laughed and talked. I wasn't afraid last year. Grade six had made me awkward. Shamini was right. We had always, *always* been best friends.

As I stood there, staring at the girl who used to be my best friend, I saw Adam and Carey heading over toward her. Little kids moved away as soon as they went by because they were pretending to swat them like flies. Why did they like picking on little kids? Did it make them feel bigger? Why would they need to feel bigger?

I pulled at Alfie's shirt and pointed to Adam and Carey.

We both stopped moving and we both stared.

"Maybe Shamini knows them," he said. "She has been hanging with a lot of grade sevens because of her soccer."

There was a weird feeling in my stomach. It kinda rumbled. Something didn't seem right.

Adam faced the girls and Carey moved behind Shamini. They definitely looked like they were up to something. What, I had no idea.

Suddenly, I saw Carey pinch at Shamini's back. I opened my eyes wide. They were snapping her bra strap. That was awful. Poor Shamini.

She turned around and I saw the horrible look on her face. Hurt. I'd seen it before when her dog, Chester, had died. I'd seen it when her great-grandma had died. I'd seen it when she didn't make the city soccer team two summers ago.

I started running. They couldn't do that to her. It was mean and wrong. They shouldn't pick on her like that. Shamini and I *were* best friends. Always had been. And we still were. And no matter what, best friends stick up for each other.

"Hey," I yelled. "Don't do that!"

Adam and Carey turned to look at me and burst out laughing. "Here comes the shrimp of grade six to the rescue. See Doggy Diarrhea run!"

They waved their hands in the air. "Ohhhhh. We're scared." They continued laughing. "Are you pretending to be a superhero? Isn't that what you and your buddy do every day? Play superheroes?"

"Go pick on someone your own size," I said loudly. "Why do you always pick on people smaller than you?"

"Because little shrimps like you need to be taught a lesson."

Carey gave Adam a head jerk as if to say "let's teach him his lesson." Then they both swaggered toward me. "You wanna fight on the schoolyard," he said. "Cause we don't care. Give it your best shot. We'll all get suspended. Thing is, I like being suspended."

"I don't wanna fight," I said. I eyed them without backing down or looking away. I knew it was possible that I was going to get beat up. And badly.

"Ohhhhhh what a baby. *I don't wanna fight.*" They mocked me. And they kept walking toward me. "I bet you're scared now."

Adrenaline rushed through me. My blood felt like it was gushing through my whole body. But I wasn't going to back down. My feet refused to move, but I didn't really want to run. What they did to Shamini was wrong. What they did to everyone in the schoolyard was wrong.

"You don't scare me," I said. They actually did, but I had to say they didn't.

"It's okay, Archie." Shamini's voice sounded loud and strong.

"Shamini, it's not okay. It's not cool. It's not funny. And it's not okay."

"You're on a roll," whispered Alfie. "But you repeated yourself."

The guys moved another step forward and I tried to breathe. Okay, was I ready to get beat up? Tossed to the ground? Sent to the office? Suspended for fighting? I'd already been spared once.

I stood still. But then suddenly I felt bodies beside me. I turned to see Dylan and Sam standing on either side of me. Where'd they come from?

"He's right," said Dylan. "You just like making people feel little."

Man, was I glad they were beside me. It felt good to have support. Then Shamini joined us. And all her friends. And others too. Oh, and Alfie.

"What is this — a line of losers? A line of little grade six whiners." Adam rolled his eyes. "Let's leave them to their whining." He made air quotation marks when he said the word 'whining.'

They walked away. I watched their backs. When they were gone I started to shake. Like totally tremble. Whatever had given me strength and kept me going fizzled and vanished. I felt like . . . me . . . Archie, again. Although maybe I didn't.

I had stuck up for my friend. Maybe I was bigger and stronger than I thought. Just in a different way.

"That was amazing." Dylan slapped me on the back. "I didn't think you had it in you."

"You stood up to those guys," said Sam. "Like really stood up to them."

"And you did it without superhuman powers," said Alfie. "You're like a hero without being a superhero!"

"Archie," said Shamini. "Thanks."

I looked at her and held up my fist. She bumped it with hers and we did our hip hop groove and laughed.

CHAPTER NINETEEN

FUN WITHOUT TRYING

The grade six dance was on a Thursday after school. All sports teams had been given the night off and most of us had worn kinda nice clothes to school so we would look good. I had on my best jeans and the shirt I'd worn to dinner the night I ate too much. My mother had washed the entire outfit for me.

Shamini and I walked in together. She had asked me why I thought she wouldn't want to go with me. That was crazy thinking, she told me. She said we were best friends and we had a deal. She said of course we would still go together. Well, now that I wasn't acting weird anymore.

Shamini wore jeans too and a green top that was kind of swirly. My mom would say flouncy. I don't even think that's a word.

Music blared from speakers. Balloons floated from tables that were set up in the gym. Lopsided streamers were swirled and taped to the walls. A punch bowl and glasses of water were set up on a table that also had chips and pretzels.

Parents and teachers swarmed around like bees, making sure no one was bringing in anything they weren't supposed to. And also making sure no one was off in the corner doing what they weren't supposed to. Grade sevens and eights were not allowed to attend. For that I was thankful, although Adam and Carey had stopped bugging me. I had convinced my mother that chaperoning at the dance wasn't a very good volunteer thing to do. She wasn't really the volunteer mom type anyway.

"What time is your meet this weekend?" Shamini asked me.

She was talking about my wrestling meet. My first one. I have to admit I was excited and nervous all at the same time. We'd been practising for three weeks and I'd learned a pin and a throw and a few other moves. Yes, Alfie joined too. Mrs. Golden thought I had talent. At least that's what she said. And Mr. Golden, the great wrestler, said I was lucky to be small. In wrestling that could be a good thing. I actually liked him a lot, even if he was my teacher's husband. He reminded me of my grandpa.

"I think I have my first match at 10:30," I replied to Shamini.

"I should be able to make it," she said. "Are you nervous?"

"So nervous," I said. "I've never done anything like it before."

"You'll be great."

A fast song blared through the speakers. "I love this song," she said, moving her shoulders. "Let's dance."

"I'm not a very good dancer," I said.

"Who cares? Just move your feet."

Alfie slid across the floor, bashing into us.

"Alfie!" Shamini squealed.

He was wearing a pair of white shoes, like men's fancy shoes, so he could slide across the floor. He'd told us that's how he danced. They were shoes from the summer wedding he had to go to. "Let's rock and roll," he said, making moves that made him look like a fish flapping its tail.

"You're too funny," said Shamini.

We made our way to the dance floor. I was bad. But Alfie was worse. Even though he thought he was better. I moved either my arms or my legs, but not both at the same time. He just spun around and around until he was almost dizzy. Dylan and Sam joined us. It didn't bother me one bit because they were pretty bad dancers too. And so did Naomi. But she didn't dance with Alfie, which was a good thing. The way his arms and legs were moving, she might get hurt.

We all danced together, one song after another, until I was sweating like crazy. It was like a leaky tap was dripping down my back.

"Let's take a break and get a drink," said Shamini.

We walked over to the table where the drinks and snacks were. "This is so fun," she said.

"Yeah," I replied. "It is."

And it was fun without trying. I could just be me, even if I was a bad dancer. Even if I was shorter than anyone else at the dance. Well, except Susie Wong.

Maybe grade six wasn't so bad after all.

Acknowledgements

Enormous thanks to Lorimer for giving me a chance to write humour. It felt so amazing to be trying something new, to be working my brain. I had moments of doubt when I was putting the words on the page but Kat, my editor extraordinaire, was always there to help and answer questions and give advice. Oh, yes, give advice. I needed it too. The Lorimer team did a great job of the cover and the insides to give it that fun appeal. The idea came from my son, because he was one of the small ones in grade six. I remember his efforts to get bigger, none of which worked. So . . . thanks to him for giving me material. And to my readers, please enjoy Archie and his efforts and know he succeeded in the end no matter what his size. Laugh, it's good for you!